This book belongs to:

_____

_____

For Team McCallum:
Ben, Toby, Ella and Charlie.

Text copyright © 2010 Jill Newton
Illustrations copyright © 2010 Jill Newton
Dual language text copyright © 2010 Mantra Lingua
Audio copyright © 2010 Mantra Lingua
This edition 2013

Mantra Lingua
Global House
303 Ballards Lane
London, N12 8NP
www.mantralingua.com

# 森林运动会

# SPORTS DAY IN THE JUNGLE

## Jill Newton

*Mandarin translation by Minmin Chen*

森林即将举行运动会，
动物们都在忙着练习。
嗯，*几乎* 所有的动物。

It was nearly time for the
jungle games, and every
animal was busy practising.

Well, *almost* every animal.

树懒熊懒洋洋地在树枝上观望，
他动也不动。

Sloth slowly watched from his
branch. He didn't move very much.

猴子从他身旁荡过。
"树懒熊，快看我！来抓我呀！"

Monkey swung past.
"Look at me, Sloth! Try and catch me!"

树懒熊看着猴子在树丛中消失 …

… 然后叹了一口气。

Sloth watched Monkey
disappear into the trees…

…and sighed.

他看着狐猴跳跃，
黑豹飞扑，
长臂猿在 密林中杂耍。

He watched lemurs leap,
panthers pounce
and orangutans do the jungle juggle.

而树懒熊慢慢地 …
慢慢地 …
慢慢地闭上了眼睛。

And Sloth slowly...
slowly...
slowly closed his eyes.

"树懒熊，
你抓不到我！"
猴子笑着说。

"You can't catch me, Sloth!"
Monkey laughed.

树懒熊望着猴子在树枝间飞旋，向着分队处荡过去 …
然后叹了一口气。

Sloth watched Monkey spin about on the branches, swinging off to the team selections...
*and sighed.*

豺狼在旁边看到动物们都在尽显所能。
她首先选了猴子，因为猴子*总是* 胜出。

Jackal looked on as every creature tried its best.
She chose Monkey first as Monkey *always* won.

没有人选树懒熊，因为
比赛不需要无所事事
的本领。

Nobody chose Sloth.
There was no race for
hanging about.

各个队伍都在齐心协力地努力着。
他们都*很*想在森林运动会中夺冠。

The team
worked hard.
They all really
wanted to win
the jungle
games.

"我会赢的！"猴子叫道，
"没有人能够追到我！"
所有的动物都看着猴子 …
然后叹了一口气。

"I'm going to win!" called Monkey.
"No one can catch me!"
All the animals watched Monkey… and sighed.

经过一个漫长而焦躁不安的夜晚，太阳终于出来了，各个参赛队伍也出来了，

森林里一派 生机勃勃 的运动景象。

After a long, restless night the sun finally appeared. And along with it came the competing teams.

The jungle was alive with sport.

树懒熊慢慢地转移到另一棵
树枝去看老虎打滚，
看巨嘴鸟跳探戈；看大象打斗，
看青蛙
蹦来
　　蹦去　　地跳跃。

Slowly, Sloth moved branch to watch the tigers tumble, the toucans tango, the elephants humph and the frogs hop,
skip and jump!

很快便剩下最后一场比赛了。

"这个小菜一碟，"猴子一面做好准备一面说道，"我飞快如风，没有人，*我是说没有一个人*，能追得上我！"

Soon there was only one race left.
"It'll be a breeze," said Monkey as he got ready.
"I'm as fast as the wind. No one, *I mean no one*, can catch me!"

猴子从大树干飞跳到小树枝，
再向树藤跃去，荡得越来越快，
大家都高声欢呼，因为他与其他比赛对手的距离

越来

越远。

Monkey raced from bough to branch to vine,
swinging faster and faster.
Everyone cheered as the gap    got      wider.

猴子纵身一跃抓住了最高的树梢 …

Monkey leapt and grabbed the
highest branch of the tree…

树懒熊慢慢地 …
慢慢地 …
慢慢地从他的树枝上站起来，

Sloth slowly…
slowly…
slowly stood up on his branch.

他伸出长长的胳膊，
然后 …

嗖地一下！

He stretched his long arms,
then…

WHOOSH!

树懒熊最终抓住了猴子，
所有人都欢呼喝彩。

Everyone cheered as
Sloth finally caught
Monkey!

# JUNGLE FACTS

Sloths are surprisingly good at swimming

Lemurs use their big tails to signal to each other

Panthers are really good at climbing trees

When a male and female toucan like each other they use their beaks to throw fruit to each other

Elephants make lots of interesting noises They grunt, purr, bellow, whistle and trumpet.

Monkeys live in groups called troops.

A tiger's roar can be heard more than a mile away

If people don't stop chopping down the jungle, very soon there won't be any jungle left.